Here Comes
Shopkeeper Hippo

Jonathan London
ILLUSTRATED BY Gilles Eduar

ASTRA YOUNG READERS
AN IMPRINT OF ASTRA BOOKS FOR YOUNG READERS
New York

For Sean and Steph, Naiya, Aaron, Heather, Willa Rose, and sweet Maureen
—JL

For Vitor FM
—GE

Text copyright © 2023 by Jonathan London
Illustrations copyright © 2023 by Gilles Eduar
All rights reserved. Copying or digitizing this book for storage, display, or distribution in any other medium is strictly prohibited.

For information about permission to reproduce selections from this book, please contact permissions@astrapublishinghouse.com.

Astra Young Readers
An imprint of Astra Books for Young Readers, a division of Astra Publishing House
astrapublishinghouse.com
Printed in China

ISBN: 978-1-63592-593-7 (hc)
ISBN: 978-1-63592-594-4 (eBook)
Library of Congress Control Number: 2022921816

First edition

10 9 8 7 6 5 4 3 2 1

Design by Symon Chow
The text is set in BaileywickJF.
The illustrations are done in gouache and finished digitally.

Little Hippo didn't like being little. In fact, he liked to dress up and pretend that he was big. So one day, he marched off to play shopkeeper, pulling his little red wagon filled with items from home—
squeakidy-squeak . . . squeakidy-squeak.

"Here you go," said Shopkeeper Hippo. "Five cents!" Ostrich put on the sunglasses, smiled brightly, and gave Shopkeeper Hippo a nickel. Shopkeeper Hippo dropped it into his cash register—

ka-CHING!

"Thank you!" said Shopkeeper Hippo. *"Please come again!"*

"I DON'T HAVE FIVE CENTS!" roared Giant Crocodile.
"BUT I'LL GIVE YOU A FREE SHOWER!"
He snapped up the mask and snorkel, plunged back into the river—
SPLASH!— and with a great swish of his tail—

—gave Shopkeeper Hippo a free shower! Then Giant Crocodile swam off, going bubbly-bubbly, toot-toot! spurting water from his snorkel.

"*Uhhh*, thank you!" called Shopkeeper Hippo, dripping wet. "Please come again—but not *TOO* soon!"

Next, he moved shop—squeakidy-squeak... squeakidy-squeak—and along came Long Neck Giraffe.

"Hello! I am Shopkeeper Hippo! How can I help you?"
"*Hmmm*," said Long Neck Giraffe. "I would like that handsome scarf, please!"

"Here you go," said Shopkeeper Hippo. "Five cents!"
Long Neck Giraffe slowly lowered his very long neck

down . . .
    down . . .
        down.

Shopkeeper Hippo picked a nickel from the giraffe's leather pouch and dropped it into his cash register—ka-CHING! But surprisingly . . .

. . . the scarf fluttered away in the wind—
WHOOSH!—and Long Neck Giraffe galloped
after it—*galumph! galumph!*

"THANK YOU!" shouted Shopkeeper Hippo.
"*Please come again!*"

Once again, Shopkeeper Hippo moved shop—
squeakidy-squeak... squeakidy-squeak—
and Graceful Gazelle galloped up.
"Hello! I am Shopkeeper Hippo! How can I help you?"
"Oh!" said Graceful Gazelle. "I would like that colorful Frisbee please!"

Shopkeeper Hippo walked and walked in the warm shade—squeakidy-squeak . . . squeakidy-squeak—and finding a good spot he set up shop.
Suddenly, he heard a branch snap. Out bounded . . . *LION!*
"Yiiiiikes!"

"Um, um, um . . ." muttered Shopkeeper Hippo, "I mean, how can I help you?"
Lion bared his long, sharp teeth and growled, "Do you have anything . . . *tasty* to eat?"
He licked his lips, squinting his eyes down at Shopkeeper Hippo.

Shopkeeper Hippo shivered . . . but he stood up tall.
"How about this, um, nice jar of jelly beans?
Just five cents!"
Lion glared and growled and opened his great jaws . . .

. . . and swallowed ALL the jellybeans in one big *GULP!*
"DEEE-LICIOUS!" roared Lion and gave Shopkeeper Hippo a nickel.
Shopkeeper Hippo dropped it into his cash register—ka-CHING!
"Thank you!" said Shopkeeper Hippo. "Please . . . uhh . . . come again!"

. . . then, after darting into Zebra's pottery store,
he prepared a secret surprise.

Little Hippo hurried a-a-a-lll the way home,
as proud as can be—
squeakidy-squeak . . . squeakidy-squeak—
and raced up to his mother.

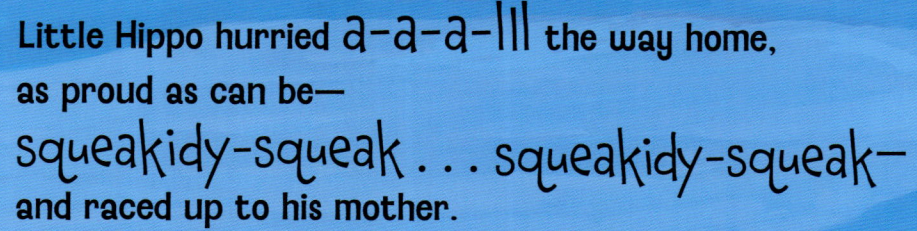

"Where have you been, Little Hippo?" asked Mama Hippo. "I've been playing Shopkeeper Hippo! I took my little red wagon everywhere and sold almost everything I had. And now . . .

". . . I have something for *you!*"
Reaching into his wagon, he pulled out the secret surprise.
"What beautiful tiger lilies!" cried Mama Hippo.
"And this vase is my favorite color!"

"For my *favorite* mother!" said Little Hippo, with a little giggle.

"Aaahhh," said his mother, wrapping him in a great big hug.

"From my *favorite* shopkeeper, my darling child."